For Jenny,

In memory of R.

With gratitude to the Arts Foundation for its support and to John Akomfrah, and David Upshal for the vital sparks,

and with heartfelt thanks to Tereza Brdeckova, Trevor Carter, Grigory Chartishvili, Daria Chrin, Sacha Dugdale, William Elliott, Masha Gessen, Henri Jansova, Maria Kozlovskaya, Yelena Krishtof, Julia Latynina, Milada Novakova, Martina Moravcová, Kevin O'Flynn, Sergeant Stiina Rajala, as well as all the others who so generously contributed their memories and experiences . . . and last but not least, Radka, for lending me her name.

Then I told him to let me go away from their church and I do not want to marry again, because I could not bear to be baptised with fire and hot water any longer, but when all of them heard so, they shouted, 'Since you have entered this church you are to be baptised with fire and hot water before you will get out of the church, willing or not you ought to wait and complete the baptism.' But when I heard so from them again, I exclaimed with a terrible voice that, 'I will die in their church.' So all of them exclaimed again that, 'You may die if you like, nobody knows you here.'

AMOS TUTUOLA – *My Life In The Bush Of Ghosts*

The whole people in the village saw us but as we were strange to them although they recognised us, they gathered together and were following us with wonder. They were also shouting on us as they were following us: 'Why the moneys you bring from your journey are nearly to kill you? Why? Are these lumps of iron which you carry now the moneys you bring? Wonderful.' It was like that the whole people of the village were making mockery of us.

AMOS TUTUOLA – *Ajaiyi And His Inherited Poverty*

. . . it is not that I would forbid the making of statues, shaped in marble or bronze, but that as the human face, so is its copy, futile and perishing, while the form of the mind is eternal, to be expressed, not through the alien medium of art and its material, but severally by each man in the fashion of his own life.

TACITUS – from the Epilogue of *Agricola*

Hamburg

September 1998

ONE

The two Africans in the forecourt of the Hauptbahnhof were playing an old Motown hit. One of them was standing up, strumming a battered old guitar, the other was seated cross-legged on the ground behind him, beating on a drum balanced between his knees. You could hear them all over the railway station, but it took George a long while before he could make out the tune or the words. He had heard the song a few times on the radio, but the Africans gave the melody a mournful, wailing twist which made it almost unrecognisable. George also spoke English well enough to realise that their intonation was so peculiar and their pronunciation so incorrect that they were mangling the words, running them together into lines which made no sense. Another three Africans sat alongside in a short line, open suitcases spread out in front of them stacked full of curios, carved wooden figures, necklaces and bracelets made from beads and shiny stones. All of them wore loose shirts made from printed material, cheap imitations of African cloth.

It was about lunchtime, and the station had begun to fill up with office workers making short trips. It wasn't as crowded as it had been earlier in the morning, or as it would be later during the rush of the evening, but there was a constant flurry of people coming and going. Around the margins prowled a scattering of hucksters, buskers, hawkers and hustlers; a flock of gypsy women, brown faces and heavy eyebrows shrouded in rainbow shawls, a couple of Turks selling lottery tickets, three lurking Uzbekis, swarthy and battered, red eyes darting furtively, a red-haired German youth in a tight black suit and dark glasses playing riffs on an alto sax, a middle-aged drunk with a ravaged face above his outstretched hand.

Beggars, drunks and pickpockets from all over the city gathered here, mostly because of the international traffic which flowed through its doors. To make matters worse the city's Hauptbahnhof stood a stone's throw away from the dramatic bulk of the Kunsthalle Museum, along Glockenweisserwall. In comparison the station was a drab and unattractive building, a big square rectangle of glass and ugly grey brick, having been rebuilt in the forties after Hamburg was blasted into twisted rubble by Gomorrah, the firestorm of British bombs in 1943.

It had the appearance, George thought, of a hundred other such places in the centre of Europe, like a beach where the ebb and flow of passage washed up and deposited human flotsam.

Behind him the station exploded with the noise of a new arrival, and he guessed that the train from Copenhagen had just pulled in. A minute later the buzz of voices and a flood of young tourists streamed through the forecourt, the rucksacks on their backs proclaiming their mission. A group of blonde teenage girls filed past George, pushing mountain bikes, their faces red and pink with the sun, spun-sugar hair bleached to a uniform pale yellow. As they reached the Africans, playing now with renewed vigour, they paused and stared, giggling in unison. Then one of them reached out and dropped a couple of coins on the blanket in front of the musicians before the little group moved on, wheeling their bikes down the slight incline towards the Adenauerallee.

Watching them, George felt a slight prickle of irritation. The girls had looked at the Africans with the patronising curiosity they would probably apply to all the other exotic sights they were about to see during their vacation. Part of what he felt was embarrassment for them; the other part was mainly anger. For most of his childhood, conditioned by his mother's tales, whenever he heard the

4

word Africa or the name of particular African countries, he had experienced a thrill of curiosity and a peculiar spike of nostalgia, as if he had been there and was now living in exile. In his heart he dreamt of sitting in the shade of a giant tree, singing strange songs, surrounded by a pure aura of effortless joy. In time the dream vanished, but somewhere inside he still had the hope that Africans would be tall and heroic presences, men whose eyes looked into far and beautiful distances. He knew now that this was also a fantasy he had manufactured out of his own longing, but, in spite of his adult understanding, he still couldn't help a swell of resentment towards Africans like the ones in front of the Hauptbahnhof. In the last few years he had seen too many of them, their breaths furred and stinking, their bodies racked with the pain and exhaustion of how far they had come, their skins and hair grey with the dread of long nights locked in the hold of a ship or a container, listening for the footsteps which might mean death. Even so they stayed alive, red eyes glistening with the lust to survive, movements swift and stealthy as rats, scuttling steadily through alien cities, from disaster to oblivion.

'*Vlasti chornim. Zamyechatyelni.*'

The voice behind him spoke one of the words which had floated through his mind, sounding like a mocking commentary on his own thoughts. A soft laugh followed, as if to underline the sarcasm. George didn't bother turning round. Only Valentin would have wanted to get under his skin by using the expression Black Power about these ragged buskers.

'*Den Mund halten,*' he muttered out of the side of his own mouth. 'Or speak German. Around here they don't like Chechens.'

This was true. On the other hand, Valentin was not from Chechnya at all. He had been part of the army of Russian conscripts which had been despatched by Yeltsin and Grachev to have the stuffing knocked out of them by the Chechens. That had been over four years ago, but it was still the worst thing that had happened to Valentin and George knew that the reference would stop him in his tracks.

'*Es ist kühl,*' Valentin said, switching to German. 'I don't like them either.'

He stood beside George, watching the Africans. He was dressed today in authentic American clothes: Levi's, Nike sneakers, and a brown Calvin Klein jacket. The Africans were droning through the same number, but he clicked his fingers like an American in the movies, trying to gee up their rhythm.

'I know this number,' he said. He spoke the title in thickly accented and halting English, but his eyes gleamed with pride at being able to do so: 'If I was carpenter.'

'That is all the English you can speak,' George told him.

'*Bullchite,*' Valentin shot back at him. 'One, two, three, four. Hello mister. I speak good.'

He looked round triumphantly, and George nodded, suddenly tired of the game.

'Where's the car?' he asked.

The car was an English model, a '96 Jaguar, which Valentin had picked up in Berlin, off the Ku'damm, early that morning.

'We're going to Altona,' he said.

'Take care then,' George told him.

'*Ja, ja,*' Valentin grunted mockingly, and shot off along the Mönckebergstrasse. The traffic was moving freely, and soon they were close to the lanes of stalls and the clutter of tourists clustering round the front of the Rathaus. George put his hand out to attract Valentin's attention and pointed towards the town hall.

'*Langsam bitte.*'

Valentin grinned in acknowledgement, but instead of cutting his speed he made a quick left turn towards the river, heading for the Landungsbrücken harbour and the road which ran up to Altona along the Elbe. All the way he kept up his inane chatter in two languages which George

6

hardly noticed. Instead he watched the city going by. The problem was that something had happened that morning on which he couldn't quite put his finger, but which had darkened his mood as effectively as if a black cloud had passed across the sky. After Berlin this was his favourite city, and in normal times he would have enjoyed the mere sensation of cruising along the waterfront anticipating the changes in the landscape that he knew like the back of his hand. First the red brick warehouses and cobblestones of the Speicherstadt, then the big green sailing ship, then the writings on the wall in the Hafenstrasse. He had walked here with his mother. In the Fischmarkt they had sat at a trestle table in the yard of a restaurant by the water's edge. At the counter nearby two fat women tossed handfuls of fresh fish in sizzling pans, and a delicious smell of frying filled the air. 'You speak to them,' his mother said. In unfamiliar places she was still nervous about the distinctive sound of her Russian accent which she had never lost. 'They're staring at me.' He had laughed, enjoying the irony. 'They're staring at *me*,' he told her. 'A black man, with a blonde beauty old enough to be his mother.' He had tickled her hand and she laughed with him, losing her self-consciousness for a moment.

As if reading his mind, Valentin spoke her name.

'Katya.'

'What?'

'I said I saw Katya last night. I went to the apartment. She wants to see you.'

George nodded. Valentin's relationship with his mother was another irritant. He had turned up a few years ago, out of the blue, a big grin on his face and a bouquet of flowers in his hand. His mother, Yelena, was dead, he had told her. This was Katya's favourite cousin from her youth in Moscow, nearly forty years previously. She had made him promise, he said, to go to her dear Katya in Berlin and cherish her. By the time George arrived, his mother seemed beside herself with delight. This was his cousin Valentin, she had informed him. He had got her address from some old letters, and arriving in Berlin had come straight to see his relatives. To George's eyes Valentin looked like any other Ivan, short, dirty blond hair, lean, a crude way of shovelling food into his mouth as he sat spreading himself at the small dining table in his mother's apartment. She had been cooking with special care that day, as George realised from the smells which struck him even before he put his key in the door. Most of the time she bought herself the cheap convenience foods she found in the nearby supermarket, stuffed chicken breasts, perhaps, frozen or easy to prepare. Sometimes, when he came to visit, all she would have to offer him was an omelette or a grilled chop. By contrast, there was an enormous bowl of borshch in front of Valentin, flanked by dark rye bread and a saucer of sour cream, which he was dolloping on to the surface of the soup in great white lumps. Dotted around the table were a heap of meatballs, a stack of blini, and a plateful of aubergines sliced, rolled and stuffed.

As George came into the room Katya looked up from the table opposite the stranger, her blonde curls, now going white, dishevelled, her cheeks pink and her eyes shining.

'Your cousin,' she called out, her voice shrill. 'Valentin Valentinovich'.

Far from being thrilled at being able to embrace this new relative, as his mother seemed to think he should be, George was angry. All he knew of his mother's family was that they had ignored her for decades, as if she was dead. She had explained to him many times how dangerous the situation had been for them all at the time when she had to leave Moscow, but he believed in his heart that it might also have been something to do with him, the baby who would grow up to be an African like his father, his colour a sign of the relationship which had marked Katya's fate. Her family had no choice, she would say, but although George knew everything she told him was true he still wanted to shout at her, to warn her to keep her distance. But it was too late.

Something about Valentin had charmed his mother silly. Her heart, as she often told George, bled daily for the days of her childhood, and for several years she had longed to return, dissuaded only by her son's opposition. Her parents had died years ago, so there was now no home to which she could return, and no one in Moscow to look after her, he would reply. Besides, he told her, life was tough there in Russia. Most Russian women like her would give their right arms to be ensconced in a comfortable apartment in the middle of Berlin, with their own friends around them, their own routine, their own welcoming cafés on the doorstep. But only for a visit, she had wheedled, so you can see the town where I grew up. One day soon, he always said. At the back of his mind was the fear that once she was in Russia he wouldn't be able to persuade her to leave.

As sometimes happened, he ended the argument by reminding her about his race. 'It's bad enough to be a German,' he told her. 'I'm not ready yet to go through the same shit in Russia.'

She accepted this without question because it was a part of his life about which she knew nothing.

For instance he hadn't set out to be a boxer, and left to his own devices he would have gone for swimming or running, but he had sealed his own fate at the age of ten in his fourth year at polytechnic school. Filing out of the classroom after a Russian lesson, Gerhard Havemann whispered in his ear, '*Schwarzer Russky*.' Almost instinctively, George had turned and punched him in the face, a good clean hit. Afterwards he could never explain to anyone why he had done something so undisciplined. '*Nekulturny*,' Katya said, in a voice of disappointment. She didn't understand any better than George himself, because the only unusual thing about what had happened was his reaction. The fact was that other children often referred to him as black and sometimes when they knew about his mother they called him 'the Russian', but there was something about the way that Gerhard put those two words together which had sparked a moment of instant and blinding rage.

What happened next was even less cultured than his mother feared. In the afternoon of the following day he was escorted to the gym where the boxers were sparring, skipping and punching a bag. In one corner the director of physical education was supervising two shadow boxers, calling out instructions as they punched and shuffled. 'Left – left – right – move your feet.'

George waited, standing to attention, wondering how they would punish him. He had been in the gym many times before, and a couple of years earlier he had been put through a couple of perfunctory lessons along with the rest of his class, more for the purposes of assessment than anything else. This was different. The boys in the room were veterans of countless competitions with other polytechnics. Some of them had been in teams which fought abroad, in places as distant as Krakow or Tbilisi, even Moscow, and it was rumoured that Kruger, the sixteen-year-old star of the school, would qualify for the Olympic trials the following year.

George rolled his eyes around, hoping to catch sight of Kruger, but in a moment the teacher turned away from his corner with his arm outstretched, the finger pointing. His eyes, a brilliant blue, seemed to be sighting along a gun barrel aimed directly at the boy. It was a typical pose. The teacher, Wolf Hauser, had been a champion middleweight in the army and he still possessed the mannerisms of a soldier, awesome and overpowering to the smaller boys. George stared back, frozen to the spot.

'You,' Hauser said. 'I hear you have a good punch. Come and show me.'

Later on, remembering the event, George had come to the conclusion that the colour of his skin had more to do with his recruitment to the boxing squad than the power of his punching. The only blacks Hauser had ever encountered were the American and African boxers he had faced in the ring. Sooner or later he would have thought of recruiting the school's solitary black pupil. If George had been older he might have refused Hauser's offer, but by the time he understood more about himself and the people around him the drill of training and fighting in competition had become a part of life. When he was conscripted his exploits in the ring were already in his file, part of the official record, and one or two members of his training unit had seen him fighting as a schoolboy in Berlin. Being known as a top sportsman saved him from the extremes of harassment and bullying, and he served out his time in one of the better tank regiments, exercising up and down Thuringia or trundling across Hungary in joint operations. During these years he began to nourish the dream of joining the Olympic squad. This wasn't a matter of love for the sport. It was as if, by some wonderful accident, his fists had given him the chance of a future which would otherwise be denied to him. He had no serious connections in the Party, and he didn't possess even a drop of German blood, but if he could fight his way into the Olympic team and survive a few rounds all the doors would open. A nice flat in Berlin, a decent car, a coaching job, and trips abroad. He could have had it all, except for what happened in his last fight, which was against an ageing middleweight from Torun, whose face must have been sculpted from stone. George had put him down eventually, but the shooting pains in his right hand told him something was wrong, and the X-rays confirmed that he had broken a bone. It was several months before he could train again, and by then his chance had gone.

His mother had never quite understood. Perhaps that was why he felt so much resentment at the fact that when Valentin turned up she was wild with happiness to embrace one of her own blood again, and they stayed up, night after night, long past her bedtime, drinking and talking together in Russian, too fluent for George to join in. He had suppressed his anger and the next day, for her sake, he had taken the man out to bars and found him somewhere to stay, steering him gently away from districts like the Savignyplatz where a loud-mouthed Russian could wind up with his face smashed.

It was then, on their second meeting, that Valentin had made his proposition. A friend back home, he said, somewhere in Belarus, he was vague about this, possessed a store of valuable objects, paintings and statues, that he wished to sell. George's immediate reaction was to laugh. He had heard all this before. Russians sold everything, like hucksters at a market, even the boots off their feet.

The trade in icons was an old story. Back at the beginning of the decade there were genuine icons to be had, but in the last half-dozen years, Russians, along with entrepreneurs from every other ethnic group in the former Union, had been distributing crudely painted bits of wood, some of them barely dry.

'You can't sell those things any more,' George said curtly. 'Nowadays the collectors go to Moscow or Petersburg and arrange their own fakes.'

Valentin shook his head impatiently.

'These are not icons, and they're real. I can show you an example.' He mentioned a name George had never heard of. 'An artist of the Peredvizhniki.' George had a vague idea that the Peredvizhniki were landscape painters.

'You brought one here? To Katya's apartment? A stolen painting?'

Valentin looked round and made a shushing sound.

'It's not stolen.'

His friend, Valentin said, had been given the paintings by some dead relative who perhaps had stolen them, or had been given them by someone who had. No one knew. But there it was, a collection of priceless works of art about which he could tell no one or sell in Russia.

George had been sceptical, until Valentin took him back to the room he had rented above a Turkish café off the Oranienstrasse in East Kreuzberg, and showed him the picture, a rectangle, about three feet by two, which was a landscape – in the foreground a field of waving corn, in the distance tucked into the bottom corner a house with a windmill beside it. It was a beautiful picture, full of detail, painted some time in the nineteenth century, George guessed, although he really knew nothing about it. In the corner scrawled below the house was the signature – Levitan.

In the end it had been surprisingly easy to find a buyer. Later on it struck him that it had been much too easy, but by then it was too late and the damage was already done.

The problem was where he'd started. Thomas Liebl. George had promised himself, when he moved across Berlin after the Wall, never to have anything more to do with some of the people who had previously been a part of his life. But when he began wondering how to dispose of Valentin's painting, Liebl's huge body lurched into his head, and although he racked his brains trying to think of an alternative, he knew all the time that he would go back. It wasn't an appealing prospect. There had been moments in his life when he pictured ripping a knife across the man's bloated belly, and although that was now a long time in the past, he still couldn't think of Liebl without a shadow of the rage and fear he used to feel then. The odd thing was that at their first meeting he'd felt nothing but amusement at seeing the man. Liebl had looked like a cartoon character, a huge version of a crudely carved wooden doll, an ovoid shape with short legs and a bulging round gut tapering upwards to a balding head over which a few strands of greasy black hair were carefully pasted.

At the time, George was managing the workers' canteen at a food processing factory in Prenzlauer Berg. In the early eighties it was a place of factories, workers' tenements, hole-in-the-wall cafés and hostels, a district where he could arrive and depart more or less unnoticed. The catering job was the sort of position he had held since he left the army; in George's mind it represented a period of waiting, a time during which he would decide what to do with himself. The problem was that he had been preparing for a career in sport since he was about fourteen, and when the door closed on that prospect he had been left with no idea what to do and practically no incentive to pursue other prospects.

On the morning that Liebl walked into his office that first time George had long outgrown his dreams of sporting stardom, but he retained the habit of weighing up other men for their potential in the boxing ring. Sometimes he would find himself gazing at someone taller than himself and wondering with which hand he would lead or how fast he was on his feet. It took only one glance to see that Liebl would be a hopeless case. One punch and he'd be down. George smiled, thinking about it, and Liebl's big moonface split in reply.

'What can I do for you?' George asked.

Liebl collapsed slowly on to one of the rusty steel chairs. George's office was also a storeroom where tins of cabbage and beetroot stood piled on the floor next to the bottles of schnapps and vodka. His desk was a sturdy pine table, marked by the scratchings of generations. In one corner a carved swastika had been converted into a crude hammer and sickle. With the addition of three chairs, there was just enough space left to walk around the table and out of the door.

George laid down the sheaf of receipts he had been totting up, and faced Liebl with his arms folded, realising now that the man must have some official function.

'Thomas Liebl,' the man grunted. '*Sicherheit.*'

The word startled George.

'Security? What about Werner?'

On the previous morning he had spoken with the head of security, Werner, an easy-going veteran who had served in George's unit ten years before.

'Werner has been transferred. I'm here now.'

George's heart skipped a beat. He was certain that Werner

had not known about his own transfer, and if everything had been as normal he would have toured the place saying goodbye. The answer must be that they had brought him up in front of the factory's conflict committee in the afternoon and then kicked him out of the gates. Right now his friend would be cleaning up some filthy dump, or shovelling medical waste and body parts. Even worse, he might have been arrested. The entire affair would have had to have taken less than twenty-four hours. Flabbergasted, George was about to ask what had happened when he realised that it might be unwise to show too much interest.

'You were friends?'

Liebl was smiling again.

'We talked,' George said cautiously, 'about the army.'

He could hardly deny it.

'Did you talk about the vodka?'

This time George's stomach lurched. He had been selling cases of the stuff on the black market for over a year. It wasn't the sort of transgression which interested Werner as long as he got his regular supplies. George had always assumed that he was taking a cut from every hustle which went on in the factory. Everyone had some kind of scam working for them, and it was easy to forget that it was a crime until you were caught.

'Vodka?'

He was playing for time, but he knew he had been caught, and looking at Liebl he noticed that the curve of his fat lips wasn't a smile at all, merely a reflex expressing some kind of pain or stress. Realising this, he understood that the man was playing with him, the eyes gleaming through the folds of flesh as cruel as a cat.

'The vodka that the Poles bring you,' Liebl said, 'costs less than half the stuff you put on the books. Everyone knows that.'

That was the way things were, George wanted to reply, but he knew by now that whatever was going on was also something to do with the way things were. The truth was that the canteen swindles had been going on before he arrived and they were a part of his everyday routine. He suspected that Liebl knew this already, and he probably knew that most of the products on George's books ended up on the black market or in the kitchens of the production committee – two days earlier the manager himself had collected half a dozen bottles – but for some reason they had decided to throw him to Liebl.

'They say you're a good worker,' Liebl continued, 'and I don't want to charge you with anything.'

So all this had merely been a preamble to his real purpose, a way of letting George know that he had to give Liebl what he wanted. The question which remained in his mind was why the man hadn't simply asked for a few bottles. Werner had understood the limits. If his replacement was greedy it might cause problems.

'What do you want?' George asked.

'We want you to do a job.'

Whatever it was, George thought, he wanted nothing to do with it.

'I have a job,' he said, 'and I don't want a transfer.'

'We don't want to transfer you.'

For the first time it occurred to George that Liebl wasn't simply a security officer.

'Who is we?'

'Stasi.'

At last he understood. This was the way that state security operated, and he would have to do whatever it was they wanted.

At the beginning it was easier than he would ever have imagined. Liebl wanted to know about the black market, where the products came from, where they went and who handled them. Most of it he already knew. The rest he could have found out by observing what went on around the factory. George laid down ground rules. He refused to talk about his colleagues or about his mother and her job translating for Soviet officials.

16

'I respect that,' Liebl said. 'We are only concerned with the vandals who are undermining the State.'

As time went on George never trusted Liebl any more than he had that first morning, but before long he felt at ease. Liebl, he understood, wrote exhaustive reports about everything he learnt, yet little or nothing seemed to change. He had half expected some of the traders he knew to disappear, perhaps a few transfers or arrests, but things at the factory went on much as they had always done. Liebl's questions came to seem like a bit of a joke, a sort of monthly quota with which he filled his notebook. Improbably, Liebl turned out to be a boxing fan, with an encyclopaedic memory for lists of fighters from Poland, the Ukraine and Cuba. Somehow he had managed to see films of fighters like Muhammed Ali, and he revelled in describing every blow in famous matches like the Thriller in Manila. When he did this his arms flailed, his little eyes gleamed and he gasped for breath. After a while George realised that he actually liked the man, and it would have been hard for him to imagine the rage and contempt he would come to feel in Liebl's presence.

On the other hand, as he told Valentin when they began talking about what to do with the Levitan, if you wanted to sell a painting of dubious origins and ownership, it wouldn't be hard to find interested parties, but the problem was avoiding buyers who were police informers or simple thieves. If Liebl was well disposed he could send them to a buyer who was safe and would keep his mouth shut. Valentin's response was to urge him to see Liebl.

'So he was Stasi. That's much better. He will have to be quiet.'

George shrugged. Up until the moment he mentioned Liebl he had had no intention of speaking to him ever again, but when he thought about his life behind the Wall it seemed to have taken place in another world. Perhaps it was the same for the Stasi. He could still recognise people who had been in the same trade as Liebl, and it was as if, from the moment of the *Wende*, they had begun to shrink, changing subtly into ordinary individuals. There were so many of them, in fact, that most of the time no one would guess. In any case Liebl had never forced him to do anything. He had simply opened the door to the maze. George's wife Radka was the only person who knew every detail of the tasks he had performed for Liebl, but during one of the worst periods in their relationship she had accused him of using the fat man as a lightning rod for his own guilt. The remark had provoked his anger, partly because he already knew it to be true. Avoiding Liebl would make no more sense than avoiding the steps of the Gethsemanekirche in Berlin, which was where he had heard about the death of a woman he had loved.

'Perhaps it is time I saw him again,' he told Valentin after seeing the Levitan.

George hadn't actually laid eyes on the man then for at least half a dozen years, but he knew where to find him. Liebl was still in the security business, and he was still based in the centre of Prenzlauer Berg, but now he ran a firm supplying bouncers to the nightclubs that littered the district. On the same afternoon that George saw Valentin's painting he decided to take the leap, to try to lay at least one of his ghosts to rest by talking to Liebl.

He parked near the KulturBrauerei, the old Prenzlauer brewery which had hastily been converted into a cultural centre. The factory where he had worked with Liebl was only a stone's throw away, but it was now deserted with a web of scaffolding covering the building while it was being converted into something else. This was how it was all over the east of the city. More than six years after the Wall came down the noise of drilling and hammering, the smell of paint, scaffolding and a kind of scattered bustle was inescapable, but somehow the changes only served to emphasise the familiar look of the place. Alongside the splashes of renovation was the scarred brick of the tenement blocks, and it was the same with the people.

Under the short skirts and high heels, or the tight jeans and tailored jackets which had sprouted along the Schönhauser Allee, were the same scrawny bodies and sallow complexions. Everything here was slower too, as if the city itself moved to a different, more deliberate, Ossi beat. George had never noticed any of this before. Now he had to remind himself, with a little shiver of irritation, that he too was an Ossi. As a child his mother had brought him here to the rushing junction where Schönhauser Allee and Danziger Strasse met Kastanienallee and Ebenwalder Strasse. Beyond was the Wall which marked the border where he should never go, she said, but at the time, the warning had been unnecessary. The spot where they stood, it seemed, was like the centre of the world, a teeming and sophisticated metropolis.

He crossed the junction and passed between steel pillars into the shadow of the railway overhead. In a couple of minutes he was walking down the cobbled street where Liebl's office was situated. Up ahead he could see the neon sign above a narrow shopfront – *Experte Sicherheit*.

He pushed open the door, which set off an electronic buzzer. The reception was a shallow room a few metres long. Against one wall was a polished wooden desk behind which sat a woman whose hair was an extravagantly pale yellow, swept back into a bun. She was wearing a turquoise suit over a tight black sweater with a low vee which showed a swelling cleavage. Her long fingernails were turquoise, matching the colour of the suit. In her left hand she held a kingsized cigarette in a stainless steel holder. With her right hand she pecked at the keyboard of the computer terminal in front of her. Against the wall opposite were two screens covered with photographs, one of them a large portrait of Liebl, his jowls arranged into a serious and responsible expression. The others looked like a series of scenes of his bodyguards surrounding important people or blocking the entrances to various venues. Between the desk and the screens was a door which

George assumed led to an inner office and the stairs to the upper floors.

'I want to see Herr Liebl,' he told the receptionist.

'You have an appointment?'

'No. My name is George Coker. Tell him I want to see him.'

She looked him over coldly before making up her mind.

'He's not interviewing today, and we don't employ foreigners. Write him a letter with a photograph, references from your former employers and proof of national status.'

'I don't want a job,' George said patiently. 'Tell him my name and tell him I want to speak with him.'

She had deep-set green eyes and a small mouth with pouting scarlet lips. The mouth twisted and the eyes fixed in a scornful glare.

'What is your business?'

'I'm an old friend,' George told her. 'From Lichtenberg.'

This was a measure of his irritation. Lichtenberg was where the Stasi headquarters had been situated, and he was guessing that whether or not the receptionist knew about Liebl's past, the mere mention of the place would bring the conversation to an end.

She laid the cigarette in an ashtray, her eyes still fixed on him, then she got up, smoothed her turquoise skirt down carefully, walked over to the door, and went out, closing it behind her. George waited, his annoyance compounded by the delay. Suddenly the door opened and the receptionist emerged, hurrying a little.

'Please,' she said. 'Go in. Go in.'

She pointed to the corridor behind her. On the far side was another open door. George noted that her manner had changed. Now she remained standing, closer to him, and there was something apologetic about the way she waved him through.

Liebl was sitting in the centre of a room in a big red leather armchair. Opposite him was a huge television set, the largest that George had ever seen. On the screen was

20

a recording of two fighters jabbing at each other under the Olympic logo. George had never seen the match but he recognised the boxer Liebl was watching. Theofilio Stevenson.

Liebl lifted his hand and the picture froze on Stevenson in a characteristic pose, his arms down, his head slightly inclined, an ironic twist to his smooth features, his unshakable confidence like an aura.

'I was watching Stevenson and thinking of you,' Liebl said. 'You always reminded me of him.'

'Thank you,' George replied, 'but I don't think so.'

He sat on the leather sofa opposite Liebl. There was a table in the corner beside the long windows which looked out on to a small courtyard at the back. The walls were a pale green colour, dotted with more photographs of Liebl, bodyguards, and clubs. Some of the photos were signed portraits. George guessed they were foreign celebrities, but he didn't recognise any of them.

'The last time we spoke,' Liebl said, 'you threatened to kill me.'

'You don't need to worry. That was a long time ago.'

Liebl made a gasping sound which, George remembered, signalled his amusement.

'If I had been worried you wouldn't be here.'

Liebl hadn't changed much, George thought, except that his head was now completely bald and he was a little thinner. It was clear also that he was making money out of whatever he was doing. At the factory he used to bulge out of the clothes he wore. Now his suit draped softly round him, giving him the well-tailored air of a pink-fleshed Wessi politician.

'You've done well,' George remarked.

Liebl took his eyes away from the TV screen and looked at him grinning as if he knew exactly what George was thinking.

After reunification a lot of people had half expected the Genossi, old comrades like Liebl, to disappear, or at least to be barred somehow from the new world. A few had been prosecuted, a few of the most prominent had committed suicide, but many of them were still flourishing, in precisely the same sort of occupation they had pursued under the patronage of the state. Often, they had managed the transition by banding in cliques, small groups the Ossis dubbed *Seilschaften*, after the teams which roped themselves together to climb steep rockfaces. Looking round Liebl's office, George was willing to bet that among the members of his *Seilschaft* there were men who owned nightclubs and promoted pop concerts.

'It wasn't so difficult to adjust,' Liebl said. He shifted his balance in the chair so that he could look into George's face. 'Why are you here?'

'I need a name.'

Liebl raised his eyebrows, the two bushy clumps of hair giving the impression of crawling upwards towards his naked scalp. Without pausing George went on to explain that he had a valuable object which had to be sold discreetly, to someone who would have the ready cash.

'How much?' Liebl interrupted.

George plucked a figure out of the air.

'Ten, maybe fifteen thousand marks.'

'Show it to me.'

'No.'

George had replied without thinking. Now that he was talking to Liebl he felt none of the boiling rage which he had associated with him for so long, and he had the odd feeling that the man in front of him was somehow different, an impostor who had been substituted for the person he had known. At the same time he knew that he could never do business with the man.

'Why do you come to me?'

'Because you can tell me what I want to know.'

'I know this,' Liebl said seriously, 'but why should I help you?'

A memory flashed through George's mind. It was a

touch, the soft smooth feel of hair, black and glossy like a bird's wing. At the back of his mind was the crazy thought that perhaps Liebl might want to atone somehow, to make up for the things he'd done. The other thing was that they'd almost been friends at one point, and if Liebl hadn't been what he was, perhaps they would have.

'The same reason I used to help you,' George replied. 'Call it payback.'

'You can't threaten me,' Liebl told him. 'Everyone's read the files.'

This wasn't true and they both knew it. At the moment that the students were hacking at the Wall many of the files were burning in the courtyards of the complex in Frankfurter Allee.

'So call it business,' George told him.

'Ten per cent,' Liebl said.

Later that evening Liebl telephoned with the name of a dealer he said was reliable. He owned a shop off the Dresdenstrasse which sold antiques and memorabilia. It wasn't far from where Valentin lived and they went there the next day.

The place was tiny, sandwiched in between a dingy pizza parlour and a video market. When the door opened it set off an electronic chiming somewhere inside, but it was difficult to tell the source of the sound, because the shop was crammed with objects, old furniture stacked up the walls, stuffed birds mounted in transparent bells, heaps of uniforms in neat piles, a giant bear skin, and a line of glass cases displaying coins and jewellery. Standing motionless behind them was a small man wearing a beard and a black Armani suit, and for a moment George had the feeling that this was another exhibit.

'Gunther?'

The man nodded.

'We spoke. On the telephone,' George said.

The dealer nodded again, then came from behind the counter, squeezed past George and locked the door.

23

'You have something to show me?'

Valentin was carrying the painting wrapped in a copy of the *Tagespiegel*, and he tore the pages away carefully before propping it up on the counter. The dealer studied it without expression. After half a minute he touched the signature with his finger, grunted softly, and went back to looking at the painting. Valentin raised his eyebrows at George, who ignored him. The shop seemed to be holding its breath.

'*Wieviel?*' Valentin said suddenly, losing patience.

The dealer didn't answer, and he didn't move.

'How much? How much?' Valentin repeated.

The dealer looked at him, smiling.

'Russian?'

Valentin stared back at him, unsettled by the question. In this city the Russians had no friends, and it must have been obvious what he was.

'I am Russian,' he said irritably. 'The painting is Russian. How much?'

The dealer smiled again.

'Five thousand marks.'

'That is shit,' George told him. 'This is by Levitan, a great painting of the nineteenth century.' He had determined to refuse the first offer in any case, but he also guessed that if the painting was genuine, this was a derisory sum. The dealer shrugged.

'A minor work, probably very early, or a fake. His best work is in Moscow or the museum at Plyos. But he was a great painter. You are right. So take it to a gallery, then. Go to Dahlem.'

He laughed, and for a moment George felt like hitting him in the middle of the tuft on his chin. Dahlem was where the big galleries were, but a black man who showed up trying to sell a painting which had no documentation would be looking for trouble. As the thought crossed his mind, it struck him that the dealer was needling them, subtly and deliberately. After all this was only the start of what might turn out to be an extended negotiation. Losing his temper would simply hand the initiative to the other man. The realisation was like a dash of cold water, and he forced himself to smile.

'It's genuine,' he repeated.

Half an hour later they had struck the bargain. Gunther upped his offer by another two thousand marks, and as if to sweeten the deal he told them, as he counted out the money, that he would take as many of the paintings as George could deliver. If they had a regular pipeline and once the market had been locked up he could pay five, maybe ten times as much. Valentin voiced no objections but, once outside the shop, he looked at George and made a face of alarm. It would be, he said, a difficult business to locate the other paintings and bring them out.

'I should have guessed,' George said. 'You're full of shit.'

At this point they were walking side by side up the Dresdenstrasse towards the bustle of the Oranienstrasse. Valentin stopped abruptly, and when George looked back he was standing in the middle of the pavement, glaring, his face crimson under the yellow hair which, in the last few days had begun to sprout in a peak over his forehead. George gestured, on the verge of apologising, but his cousin, instead of responding, spat out one word – 'mershavets'. George had a dim memory of having heard the word before, but he wasn't sure what it meant and while he was working out that his cousin had called him a bastard Valentin turned his back and walked the other way.

It was another fortnight before George laid eyes on him again. During that time he had to withstand Katya's anxious enquiries about what had happened to Valentin, why he hadn't been to visit. Under pressure he went to the room in East Kreuzberg half a dozen times without catching sight of his cousin. None of the other tenants knew anything or would even admit to having seen him, and eventually George gave up. Perhaps, he told Katya, ignoring the hurt look in her eyes, her dear nephew had seen enough of Berlin and had gone back to Moscow.

It was shortly after this that Valentin turned up. It was like a replay of the first time, Katya hovering by the dining room table, while the Russian sat grinning and stuffing his face. He greeted George like a long lost brother, making no reference to their last meeting, and while he ate and drank and smacked his lips, he found time to tell George that the business which prompted his trip back to Russia had been successful.

They left the apartment together, Katya clucking like a mother hen and pretending to scold Valentin for disappearing without a word. In the street he told George that he had returned with a deal which would make them rich men. It was simple: cars for pictures. Germany was full of cars for which there were Russian buyers. Instead of money they would receive a stream of pictures which were worth many times the price of the average luxury car.

'I've heard about these good deals before,' George told him. 'You can't lose. Next thing you know you're wearing handcuffs like they were a new fashion accessory.'

Valentin laughed, seemingly unworried by the prospect. He threw his arm around George's shoulders. 'You'll change your mind when I tell you.'

George listened, sceptical at first, then seized by a mounting excitement as his cousin told him the story.

Valentin had been offered the first picture from a former comrade in his regiment of paratroopers, with instructions to sell it in the West. He assumed it had been stolen, but when he returned with a fistful of foreign currency, his friend Victor revealed that he was sitting on a bonanza which would make them rich men. Its source, he said, went back several years to the crumbling of the Union at the beginning of the decade.

At the time Victor's company had been led by a distant relative of Colonel General Rodionov, commander of the TransCaucasus military region. Throughout the late eighties and early nineties, Rodionov had been engaged in brushfire operations in places like Armenia and Azerbaijan, not to mention the running sore of Abhazian attempts to secede from Georgia. Whenever there was trouble he sent for the paratroopers from Moscow to beef up the local *speznatz*. Victor had found himself in quick succession serving in all of these places, cracking heads, carrying sandbags to shore up riverbanks, distributing food and medical supplies. It had started after the Armenian earthquake in '88. Victor was in the ruins of Spitak, running after the sniffer dogs as they scrabbled in the rubble, pulling aside blocks of masonry with his bare hands, his throat dry and aching, his head ringing with the cries of children. Some time in the afternoon he looked up and saw Gorbachev walking towards him. At first he thought it was some kind of hallucination, then he saw the Colonel General, whom he recognised from parades, followed by an entourage of photographers, snapping the party of dignitaries. As they came abreast of him, Gorbachev paused, took off his hat, pulled out a snow-white handkerchief and wiped the tears from his eyes.

Victor was nineteen years old and something changed at that moment. Up to that time the scene which surrounded him, the agonising sight of crushed and broken limbs, the squelching mud, the smell of rotting bodies, all this had been part of the daily fare which as a soldier he was proud to withstand. Suddenly, like the flickering shade cast by a passing cloud, a kind of sorrow touched his soul.

When the unit pulled out from Yerevan the boys took everything they could lay their hands on, but one of the trucks was loaded by Victor and a couple of comrades, supervised by the company commander himself. It contained pictures and sculptures which the commander had been collecting from museums and houses which had been flattened by the earthquake. Most of the time there was no one left alive to claim these objects and the soldiers had simply picked them up and walked off without interference. After the journey back Victor drove the truck west along the Moskva to a *dacha* young Rodionov had bought at the far end of a village on the banks of the Setun. He made the trip a few more times during the next four years, content with the assurance that when the time came he would receive a fair share of the profits. Sometimes he got to keep some of the loot – gold bangles and rings or silverware which couldn't be traced. During that period a small group within the company had evolved into a sort of unofficial bodyguard who travelled everywhere with the commander: Yerevan, the Black Sea, Tbilisi. Chechnya was to be Victor's last mission, and he was sitting in front of Grozny in an armoured personnel carrier along with the other veterans when they were hit by a hail of armour-piercing grenades which the partisans had bought from a Russian conscript the previous week. Young Rodionov died instantly, and Victor found himself wandering in the wreckage of the armoured column, the only remaining member of the 'bodyguard'.

Back in Moscow he lost no time in visiting the *dacha*. The treasure was stored in a cabin near the house, and working feverishly over the space of four nights he removed everything he found there. He piled them up in the attic of the old house in Uglich on the Volga, where his aged parents still lived. Over the next few years he sold the least valuable objects piece by piece. Eventually he ran into Valentin by accident, as they were both standing in a queue for changing currency in a booth at the end of Ulitsa Vavarka. They had first met in what seemed like another lifetime, during the week before the advance on Grozny, and they began talking, hesitantly at first, then with increasing passion and nostalgia. Victor talked about the explosion and the shock of waking up to find all his closest comrades dead or maimed. Valentin told about how they had taken Grozny, then scoured the countryside, alternately frozen with the cold and sweating with fear, nothing but *kasha* porridge and bread in their stomachs, wincing from the anticipated sting of snipers' bullets, torn apart with anger at the pointlessness of it all.

By this time they were standing in front of a stall on the site of the old market place near Arbatskaya Metro, clinking their glasses together and toasting their chief tormentors. 'Yeltsin – *alkash*. Grachev – *doorak*.' These were their ironic salutes to the old boozer and the moron who had sent them to hell without the slightest idea of what they were doing.

A dam had burst. Valentin talked about his mother's death and his imminent departure for Berlin, and Victor was struck by the idea that here was the perfect conduit, a comrade he could trust to do business for him in the West.

The following evening, they met again at the apartment in the block near Belorussia Station where Valentin's mother had lived. Victor had brought the picture in the back of his van, covered with sheets of newspaper tied on with string, and, once upstairs, he propped it up against the wall on a chair and tore the paper off.

'Look,' he said, 'isn't it beautiful?'

When his cousin got to this part of the story George nodded his head, his imagination replaying the entire scene.

'Yes,' he muttered, almost as if he was talking to himself. 'It's beautiful.'

That was how it had begun.

On that first day George had asked the obvious question. Why bother with stealing cars?

'It's a cover,' Valentin explained patiently. Victor could run a more or less legitimate business dealing in taxis, cars, and car parts. No one would ask questions about his money.

'But they're stolen cars,' George protested.

Valentin shrugged.

'Who cares?'

On the morning that Valentin stole the Jaguar they had

29

been in business for nearly two years and there was still no sign of the supply of paintings drying up. The cars were no problem. Valentin had become an expert in choosing the right models – BMWs, Jaguars, Porsches, the occasional top-of-the-range Volkswagen. The streets seemed to flow with the rich, hot scent of their shining metal, sweetened by luxurious spicy touches of leather and rubber; and there was practically no risk apart from the actual moment of opening a door. When Valentin climbed into a motor in the morning he knew that by nightfall it would have travelled a distance of more than a thousand kilometres and across several borders. This was his only regret, he told George. Sometimes the pleasure he experienced when he sat in front of the wheel of a beautiful car was almost as good as sex, and when he drove it into one of the garages they used he would feel the insane desire to keep it, to remain wrapped in the clinging embrace of soft warm leather, if only for a little while longer.

'*Verrückt*,' George had muttered. 'You're crazy.' But, at the same time, he reflected that it was just as well. Their zones of responsibility had divided themselves, as it seemed, quite naturally. George's job was to sell the paintings. Valentin boosted the cars. Since their first experience with the dealer, Gunther, George had set out to inform himself about the art objects he was handling. He read catalogues and visited galleries, museums and auction rooms, checking the prices carefully, matching his estimates with them. He read about Feofan Grek, and Rublyov and Ushakov, and then leaving icons behind he read about the Wanderers group, the Peredvizhniki, Surikov and Repin, and then Mikhail Vrubel and Diaghilev. Before he had progressed very far, however, he had realised that Levitan, whose painting he had sold to Gunther for a few thousand marks, was a classic example of the nineteenth century Peredvizhniki. The landscapes were famous and highly valued, and he learnt also that there were collectors not far away who would have given him ten or twenty times the amount without a single question. 'Idiot,' he muttered to himself from time to time, as he turned the illustrated pages or sat at the back of an auction watching the bidding. 'Idiot.'

It was a new world in which George immersed himself. At first his wife Radka was puzzled, then delighted at his new-found interest. When he resigned as manager of one of the rent-a-car firms at the airport, the job he'd held down for five years, she had almost panicked, convinced that he was about to return to his old ways. But he'd surprised her with the amount he earnt buying and selling antiques, as he called them. Later on, as the stream of money swelled into something like a flood she began to worry again. But, for a while, George's happiness with his end of the bargain was complete. Valentin's adventures didn't tempt him at all. He had gone boosting with the Russian a couple of times and he hated it all, the rush of excitement as they approached the car, the sucking dread of a humiliating arrest, the stupid babbling euphoria of the escape. George was content to leave that side of the business to his cousin, and when Valentin ran off at the mouth about cars, as he usually did, he merely listened patiently, an ironic smile curling on his lips.

As Valentin swung right climbing up MaxBreuerallee towards the Bahnhof in Altona he was telling George that the Jaguar's engine made the wrong sort of noise.

'Like a tank, except it doesn't smoke and stink of kerosene.'

'You never drove a tank,' George said automatically.

Valentin looked round at him, his expression suddenly clouded.

'I've smelt plenty.'

It was a smell George also remembered with an uncomfortable clarity. Once upon a time it had been so familiar that he could go for days without noticing it. But there was still one occasion that he associated with the smell of kerosene and the grinding rumble of the armoured engines, and Valentin's remark had made his mind leap to it, like turning the knob on a pair of binoculars and suddenly seeing a distant scene in sharp focus, as if close enough to touch.

He was in the army then, twenty years old, only a boy. His unit had been sent over the border on a mission of fraternal assistance against saboteurs and subversives. That's what they'd been told in the political briefings anyway, but no one in the unit believed it. The invasion of 1968 was nearly ten years in the past, but the boys already knew that they would face scorn and pointing fingers rather than the open arms of a grateful population. The column had made a stop near Karlovy Vary, a long way short of Prague. It was the middle of the afternoon and the sun was shining brightly. They were in no hurry, the soldiers had been told, and when the little row of armoured vehicles parked by the side of the country road, some of them went off to piss in the meadow or sprawl under the shade of the trees.

George stood leaning against a tank, smoking a cigarette. He was thinking of his mother. She had clung to him, muttering endearments, her cheeks wet with tears: '*Malcheek. Chelovechek.* My little man.' Then, after he had turned away, she gripped his elbow and brought her mouth close to his ear. 'Trust no one.'

He was one of the first to see the girls. They looked German with their fair hair and long brown legs gleaming in the sun, but he guessed that they were local. Two of them were mounted on a man's bicycle, the third trotted alongside, heads up, consciously ignoring the staring eyes of the soldiers who were getting up from the roadside and standing on tiptoe to get a good look at the girl's ass as she pumped and wriggled on the high saddle. There were a few whistles, but nothing excessive. Everyone had been warned about how to behave to the local inhabitants.

At first George thought that the girls hadn't noticed him and that they would go past without a look, but as they drew opposite him, the bicycle braked, stopped, and the two girls dismounted. Facing him across the width of the road the three looked not unlike women he had known for most of his life. The tallest, the one who had been pedalling the bicycle, wore her hair twisted into a long plait which fell over her shoulder and the breast on the right. She was sweating a little, breathing hard, her skin flushing underneath the tan.

'Negro,' she said, smiling at him, 'why are you here in our country?'

George stood frozen on the spot, unable to speak. His mind was a blank, except for the disappointment which was sweeping through his entire body. For a moment he had been gripped by a fantasy in which he lay under the trees with these three beauties, stroking their thighs and sucking at their nipples.

Without taking her eyes from his the tall girl put her hand on her crotch, above the light cloth of her dress, and moved it up and down.

'You want some, negro?'

It struck him that she spoke good German, just as they had been told the locals would, and he had heard the same invitation before, couched in exactly the same words. But her voice had deepened into a tone of anger and contempt and the expression on her face was twisted into a mask of hatred, her lips sneering and scornful. George knew what hatred and contempt looked like. He'd seen it enough, but now he was gripped by a curious and irresistible desire to know one thing. Did she hate him because he was German, or because he was a black man?

He straightened up and opened his mouth to ask, but the group leader's voice cut in before he could get the words out.

'Say nothing. That's an order. These whores are sent to provoke us.'

The girls' eyes switched to the sergeant standing behind him, and they all laughed, almost in unison, and still with the same edge of contempt.

'Go home, negro,' the tall girl said. 'Wherever you come from. And take your friends with you.'

The girls giggled in chorus, to George's ears an angry insolent sound which matched the contempt in their eyes. Then they turned and walked away, still ignoring the catcalls and whistles which now reached a crescendo as they walked the gauntlet of the soldiers' eyes. George watched them until they had gone past the end of the column, then he turned round, catching a sly smile from Muller, who was still standing behind him.

'Forget it, boy,' the sergeant said. 'That's another one of their tricks.'

That was the end of it. Some time during the night they were ordered back over the border. In the intervening years he had met and fucked a number of women who looked very much like the tall girl, including his wife Radka who was herself a Czech, but he had never forgotten that afternoon, or the heat of the sun, the sneer on the woman's face, the stink of kerosene on the tank's ticking metal.

'Ottenser Hauptstrasse,' he said now, jogging Valentin's arm and pointing.

Valentin grunted and swung away from the station into a broad street lined with kebab shops and stores faced with Turkish and Arabic lettering. A little further down the Hauptstrasse he turned off again into the network of narrow streets which linked the station and the waterfront. This was one quarter of Altona which had resisted the creeping tide of prosperous and respectable residency that had begun to take over on the other side of the station, renovating the huge old houses and spawning office buildings, new banks and wine bars. Instead, this district was still the haunt of Turks and Arabs, Africans, dockworkers and whores. Among them moved the newer outcasts – Russians, Uzbekis, Chechens, Serbs, Croats, and Kosovars, groups of waddling women, their heads wrapped in scarves, their eyes lost, shepherded by men in cracked dirty boots and knitted caps.

Valentin turned another corner and pulled up in front of a red brick building. He switched the engine off, then leant forward, opened the glove compartment, took out a gun and stuffed it into the back of his belt.

'What is that?' George asked him.

He'd recognised it immediately. It was a nine-millimetre Browning. It was years ago, but he'd seen them often enough, strapped to the waists of his American counterparts on guard duty.

Valentin shrugged.

'My gun.'

'I know it's a gun,' George said, feeling the urge to hit him. 'But first, I didn't know you had it. Second, I want to know why you're taking it with you.'

'You want me to leave it in the car?'

Valentin grinned cockily, and George took a deep breath.

'All right. You can't leave it here. But when did you get it and why?' A thought struck him. 'You've been carrying it around? Suppose the cops had pulled you?'

Valentin shrugged again, grinning.

'That would never happen.'

George sat back, getting over his surprise but determined not to leave the matter there.

'What's going on?'

Now he knew what had darkened his mood earlier on. It was Valentin. There must have been tiny clues which told him something was wrong, but his conscious mind had ignored them. The trouble was that he had got accustomed to thinking about what they were doing as a business, just as if he'd been putting on a suit in the morning and going to the office. Negotiating with Gunther and the other dealers was like that. They were, of course, sharp and mean and intent on gouging him for every pfennig they could get, but that was only business. In much the same mood, he had got used to accompanying Valentin when he exchanged cars for the goods he would peddle as if they were undertaking a simple business transaction. In all that time the half-dozen

Russians he had encountered were men who he presumed were former army buddies of his cousin. In fact they looked and behaved very much like Valentin; youngish, tough, dressed in jeans, sweaters and long coats, they greeted him without surprise, handed over their merchandise without comment and vanished.

Being ignorant of the details suited George. From the beginning he had understood that the Russian end of the business was a dangerous matter. The men who could afford to buy Victor's cars would also be violent characters, unimpressed by the niceties of business ethics. When Valentin and his comrades lowered their voices and engaged in conversation, George made a point of moving away and busying himself by examining the goods. After a year he had made his own calculations and he had figured that it would only be a matter of months before he was able to end his involvement in the business. In the meantime he would keep clear of trouble.

Sitting in the Jaguar now, looking at the grin on Valentin's face, it struck him that he must have been living in a dream, and seeing Valentin's gun had been like the sudden screeching of an electronic alarm, waking him to the realisation that he was already in a lot of trouble.

'What's going on?' he repeated.

'Self-protection,' Valentin said. His expression was suddenly sulky, the lines of his face pulling downwards like a small boy rebuked.

'You don't need a *pooshka* for that,' George said. He used the word for cannon, translating it from the language of the American movie gangsters, but what was actually running through his head was a proverb he'd heard his mother use sometimes: '*Strelyat ne pooshek po varabyam*: a cannon to shoot a sparrow.'

Valentin grinned.

'You should speak Russian more often.' This was a sarcasm, because Valentin knew very well that apart from his mother's familiar sayings George was uncomfortable venturing a sentence in the language. The smile vanished. 'But there's no sparrows in there.'

'Okay.' George was openly impatient now. 'Did you fall out with your friends? Are you expecting trouble?'

Valentin shook his head.

'Tell me.'

Valentin turned to face him.

'There was a problem. One of Victor's couriers decided to go into business for himself. He took one of the pictures and tried to sell it to some people. Georgians. Someone recognised it. By some stupid coincidence it was a picture from Tbilisi. These people spoke to Victor. They said they wanted to meet his contact in Germany. They said they wanted to talk.'

'What do they want?'

'I don't know. Some deal, maybe.'

George shook his head.

'You didn't think this was important enough to tell me?'

'What would you have done?'

'Okay. I don't know. What did you say?'

'I said they could kiss my arse.' He used the Russian word with a growl of relish – *zadnicha*.

'So what's the problem?'

Valentin took a deep breath.

'I don't think Victor gave them that message.' He hesitated. 'It's a difficult situation for him. He has the pictures hidden, but if they try to find them it's only a matter of time. Too many people know about it now. He said talk to these guys. Make a deal.'

'And they're here today?'

Valentin shrugged.

'Maybe. They said sometime soon.'

'That's why you have the gun. So you're expecting trouble.'

'Maybe. Maybe not. I don't know. I spoke with Victor last week. We arranged this exchange today. Since then nothing. No answer on the telephone.'

'Is that bad?'

'Yes.'

George thought it over.

'What do you want to do?'

'No deal.'

'What happens if we tell them that?'

Valentin gestured.

'I don't know. Maybe they make trouble for my friends. Maybe they go away. These people, they're mad.' He searched for the word. 'Unpredictable.'

'Who are they?'

Valentin gave him an irritable look.

'Who? I don't know. Businessmen. Bandits. They don't advertise.'

'I don't want to be mixed up with stuff like that,' George said quickly. 'If there's going to be trouble, let's bring it to an end. Give it up. Right now.'

Valentin sighed.

'Easier said than done.' He paused. 'There's no harm in talking to them. If they're there. If you're worried, wait here for me.'

George didn't even consider the offer. He had to know what was going to happen.

'I'm coming in.'

The giant entrance to the building was guarded by closed steel shutters. Next to it was a small metal door. Valentin rang the bell and the door opened almost immediately, as if someone had been watching them drive up. The man who stood on the other side was tall and dark. Unlike the casual style of the Russians George had met previously on these expeditions he was formally dressed in a dark grey suit with a white shirt open at the collar, and shiny black leather shoes. Somehow the sharp, elegant look of his clothes seemed strange, out of place.

Standing aside without a word he waved them through. Inside, the front of the building proved to be little more than a façade. Ahead of them was a long cabin with a concrete floor and an arching roof. The other end opened on to a courtyard beyond which was another building with a short stairway running up to a door on the first floor. The entire space was littered with cars. As his eyes adjusted to the sight, George realised that some of them were rusting bodies. Others looked almost new, resprayed and polished, as if ready to drive away.

'Where's Victor?' Valentin asked in Russian. When the man didn't answer he repeated the question in German. In reply the gatekeeper pointed towards the courtyard, making a little pushing gesture as if urging them on. Valentin shrugged and moved on, threading his way through the cars. George followed, automatically listening for any sudden moves from the man behind. Every instinct he possessed was warning him of danger, and if he'd been carrying a gun he would have had his hand on it. As it was he walked carefully, almost on tiptoe, his hands hanging loose by his sides, ready for anything.

When they got to the top of the stairs the door opened as if by a signal and a clone of the first man looked out. This one was older, his black hair streaked with grey, but he was wearing the same suit and shoes and he waved them in with exactly the same gesture. They found themselves in a big rectangular room, a bit less than fifteen metres long, George estimated. The rear wall was lined with windows through which he caught a glimpse of branches swaying, but although there were also windows at the front next to the staircase all of them were so encrusted with dirt and grime that only a dim reflection of the light outside filtered into the room.

Another man in a smart grey suit was standing next to a rough trestle table placed in the middle of the room. Victor was sitting behind it. He had the same sandy fair hair as Valentin, and once George saw him he remembered that he'd met the man a couple of times in much the same circumstances. He realised immediately, though, that this was different. Victor had shifted in his chair as they came in, but he didn't get up and he didn't meet their eyes. The man standing next to him watched them impassively, his black eyes shining through the gloom. Behind him George heard the door close and the gatekeeper's footsteps descending the stairs.

'This is Konstantine,' Victor said.

'Who the fuck is he?' Valentin asked, peering down at him, speaking as if the other man wasn't present.

'Konstantine Patiashvili,' the man uttered in a calm, even tone, and from the first syllable George's guess hardened into certainty. These were Georgians; and it wasn't only their height, colouring and dress which marked them out. George could barely understand what was being said, but he knew enough to be able to distinguish the marching rhythm and the heavily aspirated sound of Konstantine's voice from the drawl of Muscovite speech.

'What is happening, Victor?' Valentin asked.

George could feel the other man behind him and he shifted a little so that he could see him out of the corner of his eye. Then he thought to hell with it and took a good look. The Georgian was watching him impassively, hands folded in front of him. Konstantine put his hand on Victor's shoulder.

'We came to talk,' he said. 'We have a business deal for you.'

'*Zdyelka*?'

Valentin repeated the word with no particular emphasis, and Konstantine's face made a tight grimace which George took to be a smile.

'Sit down, please,' he said.

They sat on opposite sides of the table. As they sat down Konstantine looked directly at George for the first time.

'Americansky?'

George shook his head, not trusting himself to reply in Russian. Konstantine waited until it was clear that there would be no answer, then he shrugged and sat down.

40

'The paintings you stole,' he said, 'came from Tbilisi. Did you know that?'

Valentin spread his hands as if denying any knowledge. Konstantine gave a real smile this time.

'Paratroopers.' He made a nasal growl of the word. 'If you were as good at fighting as you were at being thieves you would have beaten us.'

'What do you want?' Valentin asked him.

'You've been selling our national treasures for a couple of years.' He smiled. 'Everybody is doing it. You must have made a lot of money out there. You stole that money from us.' He paused, as if waiting for a reply or some kind of justification. When Valentin didn't stir, he went on. 'But these are different times. We are businessmen, and there is an easy way of compensating us. You continue your work and from now on we'll be your partners.'

'We don't need partners.' Valentin's voice sounded calm and measured. 'We don't need this business either. You don't need us. Anyone can sell their goods in the West.'

Konstantine put his hand in his pocket and put a packet on the table. It was about the size of a small envelope.

'You can be useful in other ways,' he said. He pointed. 'Open it.'

Valentin unwrapped the package slowly. It was full of brown powder. He shook his head.

'No,' he said. 'This has been between Victor and me. Now it's finished.'

The expression on Konstantine's face changed suddenly, his features transforming in an instant into an angry snarling mask.

'It finishes when we tell you it's finished.' He shifted his gaze away from Valentin, his hot black eyes burning into George's face.

'You, *chornim*.' George wasn't sure whether or not the word was meant to be insulting, so he stopped himself from reacting. 'Look.'

For some crazy reason Konstantine was unbuttoning his

shirt. George tensed himself for an attack, but the Georgian simply opened his shirtfront, baring his chest, which was covered with a straggle of longish black hair. He'd have hair on his back and shoulders, George thought. His own skin was a smooth hairless beige colour, and the sight of Konstantine's sallow and hairy skin gave him a twinge of distaste that he could hardly conceal. The man was pointing to a spot below his prominent nipples, where George could just discern what looked like a tangle of curved white lines which he guessed were scars.

'I was on my knees in Rustaveli Prospekt when the paratroopers came. They beat us with spades. *Grooshya. Grooshya. Grooshya.*' His voice was higher and quicker as he chanted. George was beginning to follow his intonation and he noticed that he softened the G at the start of the words so that they came out sounding almost like an aitch. He pointed to his chest again. 'These are the marks. Then they sprayed us with *cheryomukha.*' He clutched his throat mimicking suffocation, his face contorted. There was nothing funny about the sight. He took his hand down and his black eyes struck at George. 'Afterwards my sister was dead, suffocated by the gas. And after that they went through the town stealing everything they could put their filthy hands on.'

'I was not there,' George said carefully.

Konstantine buttoned his shirt and straightened his collar. Then he looked up at George.

'But you must pay. Nothing is finished.'

He got up abruptly and George braced himself again.

'Stand,' Konstantine said.

George heard Valentin draw his breath in sharply and he saw that there was a gun in Konstantine's hand. They stood in unison, and immediately George felt the other Georgian come up behind him to begin patting and stroking his body. In a moment he moved on, and when he found the gun in Valentin's belt he grunted and held it up in the air.

'We'll leave you to think it over,' Konstantine said.

'You can have a committee meeting. Discuss it like good comrades.' He smiled. 'When I come back we can talk about the details.'

The two Georgians walked to the door and went out, their footsteps creaking on the stairs as they climbed down.

As soon as the door closed Victor got up and went over to the corner of the room. He knelt down and began unscrewing the floorboards. As he did this he talked rapidly, his tone urgent but somehow matter-of-fact.

'They killed Anastas and Mikhail and maybe a couple more. I don't know,' he said, 'and they intend to kill me after they make a deal with you, and after they get what they want they'll kill you.'

Valentin had got up out of his chair and was standing, leaning against the table, watching Victor intently.

'Valentin,' George called. He was struggling with the sense that this was unreal, some kind of practical joke, a performance which would come to an end if he protested. At the same time he knew that this was exactly what he had been expecting from the moment the Georgian had opened the street door.

Victor was levering up the floorboards, and George wondered for a moment whether the idea was that they should somehow escape through the gap. Valentin hadn't spoken since Konstantine had left the room, and George felt a sudden rush of anger, the urge to demand an explanation.

'Valentin,' he called out. 'What are we doing?'

'We're going to stay alive,' Valentin said tersely, without turning round. 'We were in Tbilisi. Both of us. These chicken fuckers know that.'

Victor reached inside the hole he'd made in the floor and took out a long parcel wrapped in waxy brown paper. He laid it down behind him and Valentin picked it up and ripped the paper away, revealing the blunt, stubby shape of a kalashnikov.

'Go to the window,' he told George. 'Tell me when they come.'

43

George moved towards the window, hearing as he went the familiar metallic snap as they loaded the cartridges. Down in the yard Konstantine and the other two Georgians were standing together in a huddle. They were all smoking cigarettes, a faint blue cloud eddying round them like a halo. In other circumstances, George thought, they would look like a group of office workers escaping for a break. Almost immediately Konstantine flicked his cigarette away and turned towards the stairs. George pulled back from the window.

'They're coming,' he said.

Victor and Valentin were sitting on the same side of the table, their hands out of sight.

'Sit there,' Valentin told George, pointing with his chin to the corner of the table. 'When the door opens, hit the floor.'

George sat facing Valentin and Victor. Their faces were impassive, relaxed but focused. His own hand trembled a little, and he took it off the table and gripped his thigh. Listening to Konstantine's footsteps coming up the stairs he tried to calm his nerves by thinking back to his own days as a soldier, but it had never been like this. Even sitting in a guard tower at midnight he had been part of a routine, a cog in the machinery. This was different.

The door opened slowly, Konstantine peering round it, the gun in his hand outstretched and ready, his eyes swivelling around the room, locating each of them. Gradually he shuffled into the doorway, the other two Georgians out of sight behind him.

'Stand up,' he ordered.

George hadn't moved so far, caught in a moment of indecision by the way that Konstantine had entered the room, but now, in the corner of his eye he saw a flicker on Valentin's face and, without thinking, he dived for the floor. In the same instant Valentin and Victor fired from under the table. George didn't realise what had happened immediately, because he'd been expecting the sound that the rifles made on the shooting range or out in the open across a field, the way he'd heard them in the past. Instead of the familiar stutter, the noise sounded like a deafening, percussive roar. Simultaneously, the table crashed over, banging into his calves, and, feeling the impact, he had the shocking sense that he'd been hit. In the next moment there was a whoosh of movement, so that he felt, rather than saw, Valentin hurdling over his body. He turned his head and saw his cousin, erect at the window firing a burst, his arms swinging in a short arc. Victor was kneeling in the doorway firing down into the yard. Then it stopped. George felt a hand clutch his ankle and, startled into reflex, he drew his leg up and kicked out, hitting something soft and heavy. He heard a deep, laboured groan and he sat up on the floor, looking around. The hand belonged to Konstantine. There was blood leaking from his legs and belly, flowing in gentle spurts, like water from a pipe. Victor turned away from the door, got up and stood over the Georgian.

'*Svolach*,' he grunted. '*Chort staboy*. To hell with you.'

He fired a single shot, and Konstantine's head exploded in a splatter of blood and brains, which sprayed over George's trousers, drenching them red.

'*Scheisse!*' George shouted involuntarily, pulling his legs away, and he heard Valentin laugh.

He reached the door just in time to splash a gout of vomit over the landing. Down below in the yard he could see the bodies of the other Georgians, both of them surrounded by pools of welling blood. The man who had opened the street door for them had almost reached the cover of the vaulted passageway before he was hit and he lay with arms outstretched as if trying to drag himself away from the bullets.

'Come on, George,' Valentin said behind him. 'Help us clean up this shit.'

Prague

September 1999

TWO

The first time Joseph Coker saw George he had the peculiar feeling that he was looking at a jumbled up version of himself, and, as it happened, this wasn't far from the truth. A careful observer might have noted that their skins were both the same shade of light burnt ochre, that they were roughly the same height and weight, that they had the same straight, broad nose, and the same long upper lip, with a little peak in the middle, the sort of feature that Joseph's wife had pronounced cute in the days when they first got together. Joseph must have noticed, but, oddly enough, when he looked back at his memories of that first time none of these characteristics came to mind, and, during the months which followed that first meeting, he was never quite able to admit that they looked very much alike. On the contrary what he remembered later about his first sight of George was his hair.

Perhaps he would have paid more attention if he'd been prepared for the encounter, but his only warning had been a phone call from the reception desk which came just after he had walked into the hotel room and tossed his jacket on the bed.

'Mr,' the receptionist hesitated over the pronunciation, 'Mr Cocker,' she said eventually. 'Your visitor is here.'

She put the phone down before he could ask who it was, and after a moment of indecision he shrugged the jacket back on and set out for the lobby.

The organisers had put him in a hotel 'on the outskirts' of the city, perhaps because his had been a late invitation. Most of the other film makers seemed to have been accommodated in the hotels clustered around Wenceslas Square, and at first Joseph had been irritated by the prospect of being out of touch with the action. During the odd moments when his colleagues would be dropping into the cafés to rap with the local movers and shakers, he thought, he'd be struggling out to the suburbs. On the other hand, even though he already knew it would be very different, the mental image he'd had of the city was of somewhere the size of London, where a trip to the outskirts would have taken at least an hour; but to his astonishment the drive from his hotel to the centre of Prague had been a matter of less than fifteen minutes. It had seemed shorter because he was busy looking around, trying to fix in his mind the qualities of the scene through which he was moving. He had also been nervous, anxious about how the film would be received, and what he would say afterwards.

He needn't have worried. He had imagined his film up on the screen of a cinema, with rows of upturned faces following every move, but the showing actually took place in a large room on the first floor of a building sandwiched between a hotel and a shopping mall. The audience consisted of hardly more than a dozen people, and all the way through their attention was distracted by the sound of music from somewhere outside. The problem was, as one of the organisers explained to him later on, that his film had been scheduled at the same time as *The Exorcist*. The director was in the city that day, and everyone wanted to be at the session where he would speak. Hearing this, Joseph had to admit that he would have preferred to meet the famous director rather than watch his own film once again, and he had the depressing feeling that his audience were mainly people who had not been able to secure tickets for the main event, or festival staff whose duty it was to be there.

In the circumstances, after that day's session at the festival he felt more or less relieved to be at a distance from the crowd of students, cinéastes and journalists swarming like wasps around the group of writers and directors whose films were on show. Even so, he guessed that, for some reason, one of them had managed to track him and was now lying in wait for him downstairs. The idea was curiously annoying.

In the lift he wondered about the way the receptionist had pronounced Coker. He had told them his name at the desk when he checked in, emphasising the long vowel, and he was surprised that she had found it difficult. After all it sounded not unlike Coca Cola, and that had to be one of the more familiar brand names in Prague. But Jarvis Cocker might have toured the area, or maybe his near namesake, old Joe Cocker. That would account for it. He'd recognised the voice of the receptionist, a stocky blonde whose broad features had a battered look, and he remembered that, out of all the women who worked on the desk, she was the one who spoke the most fluent English. Perhaps he'd ask her why she had said his name that way.

Stepping out of the lift he'd begun framing the words in which he would put the question, but when she saw him she merely smiled and pointed towards the far end of the lobby. Looking in that direction he saw a group of middle-aged Germans sitting together, but he'd already seen them all in the morning, or perhaps it was an exactly similar group, plump, pink and noisy, moving with a ponderous speed towards the buffet tables. He looked back at the receptionist and she pointed again. This time he followed the line of the gesture and saw an armchair next to the windows, facing away from the room. Poking over the top of it was a tuft of blond curls.

Immediately Joseph began riffling through his memory of the day, searching for a woman whose hair was cut in this dramatic style, then the head moved, turning to face him, and he saw that the curls belonged to a man. The hairstyle was actually a fairly conventional fade, with the two sides of the head cut short and the middle part fluffed up and dyed blond with an auburn undertone which he suspected was natural, since his own hair was patched with the same light streaks. In the same instant he saw that the man's skin was light brown, like his own, and it struck him that this was a black man with a white parent, like himself. Another visitor from England, he guessed. Perhaps a tourist who had seen him enter the hotel and stopped in to say hello. He must be on some kind of business, Joseph thought, because his clothes had none of the casual flavour that most of the tourists affected. Unusually, he was dressed in a neat dark suit and a white shirt with an open collar; and even with the punky hairdo, he looked stylish, almost elegant.

'Hiya man,' Joseph called out, 'what are you doing here?'

In reply the man stood up and stuck his hand out in greeting.

'Hello mister,' he said.

Joseph couldn't place the accent, and for a moment he thought it was a joke. Then, looking at the expression of polite diffidence on the man's face, it struck him that this must be a black man who belonged to the region. He felt a surge of excitement at the idea. He knew that there would be mixed-race people dotted around various parts of Europe, but meeting one made him feel a bit like an explorer encountering another one of his own kind in the middle of an uncharted wilderness.

'Hello,' Joseph said. He took the man's hand and shook it. 'How are you?' He couldn't think of anything else to say. His mind went back to the reason for the man's presence. Perhaps he'd been at the festival and was eager to meet privately with the black director from England. Joseph smiled, trying to communicate the sense of comradeship the man must have been seeking. 'Were you at the festival today? I'm Joseph Coker.'

The man smiled back at him.

'I know. I read of you in the newspaper,' he said. 'I am George Coker.'

His English seemed almost perfect, but he spoke slowly,

as if struggling to get the words right before he let them go.

'You're kidding,' Joseph said, amazed at the coincidence. No wonder the guy had come to see him. 'Same name.'

George Coker smiled, his lips twisting ironically.

'I know. My mother saw you on BBC World Service television. Your father's name is Kofi.'

Joseph grinned. This, he thought, was the closest he'd come to fame.

'He was a student in Russia,' George continued. 'Yes?'

Joseph nodded, remembering. He'd said all that when they interviewed him. At the time he'd wondered whether anyone would be interested.

'Kofi Coker,' George said slowly. 'That is my father's name also.'

'You have got to be kidding me,' Joseph replied. 'No offence, man, but this is weird.'

George frowned, as if trying to understand. Then he smiled again.

'Not weird. This is the same Kofi Coker who is my father, too. This is why I have an English name like you. You are my brother.'

George had stopped smiling and was staring at him intently, as if trying to gauge the effect of what he'd said. Joseph looked back at him steadily, noting the colour of his eyes, a light greenish brown, and his relaxed pose, left hand in his trouser pocket, the other resting casually on the armchair. Paradoxically it was his visitor's assurance which steadied Joseph, because it offered him a clue about what was happening. On the previous evening he'd been met at the airport by a thin, middle-aged woman with a twitchy neurotic manner, who described herself as his festival guide. As they drove towards the town she'd given him a rapid tour of its history and geography. At the end she offered him a few warnings, mostly about pickpockets and tricksters, who were, apparently, 'foreigners, Ukrainians, gypsies, Hungarians. Prague has many rich tourists, so they come here from the East.' As she said this her eyes glared anxiously at him from behind her horn-rimmed glasses. 'Be careful.'

Remembering her intensity, Joseph wondered how she would have reacted to George, but he was also certain that this approach had to be some variation on the kind of scam about which he'd already been warned. George had the assurance of an experienced con man, and it occurred to Joseph that, for this man to survive in this world of whites, where they still treated the dark-skinned gypsies like outcasts, some formidable skills were required. Be careful, he reminded himself. Whatever this guy wanted he'd be tough and smart and probably dangerous.

'I suppose there're thousands of Kofi Cokers in Ghana. Like in this country they're probably all named Václav or something like that. You know what I mean?' George nodded slowly, as if following his words with care. 'Your father might be named Kofi. He might even have lived in Russia. Sorry to disappoint you, man, but it doesn't mean it's the same Kofi.'

George nodded again.

'Of course,' he said. 'This is not easy to believe. For many years my mother believed that my father was in Africa. She wrote to the embassy, and to Ghana. But there was no answer. Then she saw you.'

Joseph felt himself losing patience. This was some kind of smokescreen, he was certain, but he couldn't begin to guess what the man was after.

'Bullshit,' he said tersely. 'This is bullshit. I appreciate you coming and talking to me. I really do. If you want something, tell me what it is and I'll say yes or no. But don't bullshit me, man.'

George frowned, a shade of anger in his expression.

'No bullshit, mister,' he said. He took his hand out of his pocket and held it out to Joseph. 'Look.'

Joseph took the photograph reluctantly. In that moment he already knew what he would see, and he already

54

knew, somehow, that what George had told him was true.

'What's this?'

George shrugged.

'You look.'

The photograph was faded and creased, but still clear. His father was standing on some kind of bridge with his arm round a woman. She was pretty with long fair hair and she was looking up at his dad with a broad and adoring smile on her face. Joseph brought the photo closer and studied the faces carefully. No mistake about it. He was forty years younger, but Joseph had already seen a few pictures of him at around this age. It was his dad.

'Who is this woman?' he asked George.

'My mother. Her name is Katya. This was in Moscow.'

His voice trembled a little, and Joseph avoided looking at him. He turned the photo over. There was a line of writing in Russian letters on the back and a date: 1956.

'*Vajlooblenni navzegda*. In English,' George said, pointing, 'it says true lovers always.'

Quickly, ignoring George's hesitation, Joseph thrust the photograph into his hand.

'Wait a minute,' he muttered. 'I'll be back.'

Without a pause, he turned and walked away. Behind him George said something, but he paid no attention. His head seemed, literally, to be spinning. In his mind the image of his father's face loomed. Pacing down the corridor to his room, the whirlpool settled for a few seconds and he found himself focusing on the Russian woman who had been nestling next to his dad, and whose features were, oddly, very much like those of the receptionist downstairs. She was prettier, he thought, like his mum had been, and suddenly, it struck him that she also resembled his mother. In his bedroom, in his flat in Kentish Town, there was a framed photograph of his parents in precisely the same pose, arms around each other.

In the room he sat on the bed, picked up the phone

and dialled his father's number in London. As he did this he checked the time by the electronic clock on the TV set. Seven o'clock in Prague. It would be six in London. Whatever the old man had been doing during the day he'd probably have staggered in by that time. No answer. Joseph let it ring, watching the seconds flash past in a blur of green numerals. Then he slammed the phone down.

From where he sat he could see the building site at the back of the hotel. They were rebuilding everywhere, he thought idly, even here in Holesovice, outside the central loop of the town. Typically, though, there were no workers in sight, and no signs of activity. He imagined that they must have packed in and gone home to their families, or whatever it was they did during the evening, and as if in response to his thought a sudden blare of music filled the air, blasting effortlessly through the window. He recognised it immediately. George Michael, his voice quavering under the pressure of relentless amplification.

If George Coker was telling the truth, Joseph thought, there was a great deal he didn't know about his father – he corrected himself, *their* father. Would his mother have known, and if she did, why hadn't she told him before she died?

Thinking about his mother steadied him, imposing a kind of gloomy calm on his thoughts. There could still be some rational explanation. Indeed, everything George had said could be discounted or explained away, if it hadn't been for the photograph. They could have picked up the name Kofi from the interview, and perhaps none of this would have happened if he hadn't talked about his father on television. He hadn't intended to, but when the interviewer asked him where he'd got the idea for the film, a story about his father had simply popped out.

There was something about the interviewer, too. She'd had a kind face which smiled easily and a shock of dark brown curls which had just begun to acquire a sprinkle of grey. She had arrived a few minutes late for the preview, but at the end, she had introduced herself, taking his hand and complimenting him on 'a wonderful piece of work'. She gestured. 'Those men. So much larger than life.' Something about the men in the film, she said, had touched her deeply.

Joseph nodded and smiled, feeling the dizzy pleasure which still flooded through him every time this happened. Of course, he'd been lucky in his subjects. The film was no more than a series of interviews with a group of ageing Africans who had lived in Britain shortly after the war, more than fifty years ago. After he had filmed them he found himself thinking that most of them would be dead within the next ten years, but they spoke about their lives with a vitality and charm which seemed to belong to another, more expansive age. Some of them, recounting incidents from their past, made the preview audiences rock with sympathetic laughter. After the first showing a critic from one of the broadsheets had patted him on the back and told him that it would be a hit in the documentary section on the festival circuit.

The woman at the World Service had used almost precisely the same phrase before the interview, and when the recording started Joseph talked freely and with confidence, eager to please. The film, he told her, had always been somewhere in the back of his mind, because his father had been one of those Africans who had come to Britain shortly after the end of the war as a student. After Ghana achieved independence he had become part of its diplomatic corps and studied in Moscow before eventually returning to Britain. Part of his intention, Joseph said, had been to record and to understand the experiences of men like his father and the environment in which they had lived.

His interviewer listened with a flattering attention, smiling and nodding from time to time. Afterwards she complimented him again. 'Great, great. That was really fascinating.'

At the time he had been too dazzled to remember what

he had said. Now he sat running the interview through in his mind, struggling to isolate the information that a listener might have gleaned from it about his background, and about his father's life. What he remembered best was how much he hadn't been able to say. This wasn't because the interview hadn't been long enough. On the contrary, she kept encouraging him to tell stories about the men and their experiences. At the same time she made it clear that her audience would be bored and alienated if he started to talk about the process by which the film had emerged, or about the pain and rage which it concealed. When people complimented him on the work his head spun with pleasure, but underneath his excitement he sometimes experienced a spurt of churning unease about the meaning of their words.

The truth was that the first audience who saw a rough cut of the film had received it very differently. These were the men he had interviewed and whose stories he had culled and assembled. He showed it to them in a preview cinema in Soho, and, sitting in the dark it seemed to go down well. They laughed in the right places, and sometimes they shouted with approval when someone made a telling point or told a funny story. Afterwards, as they filed out, most of them shook hands and congratulated him. The only discordant note came when one old man, Mr Mensah, a Ghanaian and a particular friend of his father, held his hand for a moment and gave him a knowing smile. 'Very clever,' he said. 'The whites will love it. You'll do well.'

Later on, alone with his father, this was the first question he asked.

'What did Mr Mensah mean by that?'

Kofi shrugged his shoulders, cutting his eyes sideways at Joseph and away again.

'Mensah is a radical. He's got his own opinions.'

In that instant Joseph knew how much his father despised what he had done. His first reaction was anger, then he wondered how to get Kofi to say what was wrong. The problem wasn't simply that his father would try to spare his feelings. He knew that Kofi and his friends were privately contemptuous of people who were governed by fear of damage to their self-conceit. 'Most of the people in the world,' he told Joseph once, 'have to live with the terror of sudden death for themselves and their children, or famine or torture. Out of my mother's eleven children I am one of three survivors and I don't know what happened to the other two. In this country they spend years weeping over a nasty remark, or because they didn't get enough love.'

On the occasions when he said such things it was clear that he was also talking about the differences between himself and Joseph's mother. There was no arguing with Kofi about this. In this respect he was like most of the black people Joseph encountered, regarding the whites and the fuss they made about their emotions as ludicrously soft, self-indulgent; and Joseph already knew that if he confessed to being hurt by the old man's reaction it would prompt a sarcastic smile.

'I really want to know how they felt about it,' he told Kofi.

The handshakes had been sincere enough, but he knew that their praise was not for what they had seen. Instead, it was a compliment on his achievement in wrestling so much from the hands of the whites. Coming from Kofi's son, a man who was almost one of themselves, it was a matter for congratulations.

'What would they feel about it?' Kofi said with an undertone of irritability in his voice 'It was a nice film.'

It was the response Joseph had feared. He could question his father all day without getting a direct answer. In comparison his mother had taught him that a direct question was to be answered directly. If someone asked about her actions or her feelings she would tell them, except on the occasions when she said, 'I don't want to talk about it.' Sometimes she said, 'None of your business.' 'I can't be bothered to beat around the bush,' she would tell Joseph.

Kofi and his friends found such behaviour irritatingly confrontational and sometimes downright rude. In their world politeness and respect demanded circumspection. To make matters worse, they had all spent most of their lives in countries like Britain, where concealing their deepest feelings and beliefs from the whites had become second nature, an instrument of their survival.

'You didn't like it,' Joseph said. 'I could tell you didn't.'

'It was okay,' Kofi replied. Then he relented a little. 'Maybe it was light. You left some things out.'

It was Joseph's turn now to be irritable, but he held his tongue; he knew precisely what his father meant. The lightness and charm of the film was the result of careful selection. Most of it was actually made up of spontaneous fragments, some of them off the cuff remarks or stories incidental to the main drift of the interview. Joseph hadn't planned it that way. The film had been commissioned as part of a television series about 'outsiders' in Britain, but Joseph had been trying to make a version of it for more than a couple of years. In a sense it was the project at which he had been working for nearly two decades, and which had started with a long interview he had conducted with his father as part of a film school exercise. From that point he had believed that the reminiscences of men like Kofi were a sort of hidden history which had to be told. Making it happen was another matter, and it took more than a dozen years, during which he worked as a TV researcher, then a film editor, attending courses in his spare time, and assiduously writing proposals and scripts which were inevitably rejected. It wasn't until his mother died that her legacy gave him the resources to set up his own company. The company consisted of himself, a computer and a rented office near King's Cross, but he was able to begin touting for work as an independent producer. The jobs were few and far between, consisting mainly of short segments of film or video for other producers' programmes, and it had taken a couple of years, but his big break came when he was asked to submit a proposal for one film in the series on outsiders. The offer wouldn't have been made, he knew, at the time when he started his first job. In those days the largest companies still patted themselves on the back when they hired a black researcher, but attitudes in the industry had changed gradually, and it was now conventional practice, in most of the less prestigious TV series, to make room for at least one black independent.

On the other hand, he was competing with another dozen hungry black producers with more or less the same experience, but the passion and detail of Joseph's proposal, in preparation for most of his career, won him the commission. In the moment that he heard the news, it was as if, having been born dumb, he had suddenly been granted the gift of speech. And when he started work he had a clear outline of what he wanted in his mind, and for a time the project seemed to be going smoothly. All of the men he contacted had a lot to say, most of it the product of long years of disappointment and frustration. In comparison, Joseph's life had been comfortable and secure, but their words stirred echoes inside him, and, sometimes, listening to some story of insult or violence he felt an outrage stronger than any of the feelings prompted by his own experiences. The first edit was an angry polemic in which the men described a hostile, oppressive society and the way they had survived it. Joseph had no doubt that it was powerful and moving, but when he showed it to the producer of the series it was obvious that she didn't share his satisfaction.

'It's a bit gloomy,' was Hattie's first comment.

She had a businesslike, almost curt manner which, he suspected, was partly to do with the fact that when she started her training, fresh from university, he was already working as a researcher. At the beginning she had been warmer. Discussing his proposal in her office for the first time she had brought him a cup of coffee and sat on the edge of her desk swinging her legs which were clad in battered jeans. It was more or less what he would have expected, given their previous acquaintance as colleagues, and she had been friendly and sympathetic, nodding as she listened, then commenting that his passion was exactly the kind of motivation the series needed. Viewing his first draft, however, she seemed to have forgotten her initial enthusiasm.

'It would be okay in a multi-cultural slot,' she said, 'but we're dealing with a general audience here. All these guys are talking in generalisations. It's too abstract. They're like experts rambling through history trying to come up with an overview. Half the time they're talking about events at which they weren't present. It's all very well going on about riots or what some politician said, but if they weren't there, what's the point?'

They were all intelligent men, he explained, who imagined they were communicating a thoughtful view of the history through which they had lived. If they made it sound impersonal it was because their own equilibrium demanded some distance between themselves and the most unpleasant events.

'Yes, yes, yes,' Hattie interrupted, 'but that's not the point. The central issue is how the audience reacts to these people. They're saying complex and difficult things. That's no problem. Let's take it for granted that their analyses are correct and they're telling the truth. It still doesn't work unless you give the audience characters with which they can sympathise and identify.'

Joseph brought out his best arguments, but there was no shifting her.

'I have a suggestion,' she said eventually. 'Do another edit. Keep the same structure, but take out every story and every statement which doesn't begin with the word I.'

Joseph went back to the drawing board, but his second effort had no more success.

'Maybe you're too close to it,' Hattie said before she left.

The next day Joseph got a message from her asking for copies of the transcripts of his interviews, and the following day she gave them back to him, several pages marked with yellow highlights.

'Try editing these in,' she said. 'Don't worry about the length. We'll bring it down later.'

The final product was a long way from the film Joseph had set out to make, but Hattie's satisfaction was infectious. His success in this project, she hinted, would make the going a lot easier when he put in for his next commission. Joseph had felt more or less vindicated, and Mr Mensah's comment after the preview in Soho was the first indication that his pleasure might have been misplaced.

That afternoon he sat watching the film, spooling back to see various sections and trying to separate himself from it for long enough to gauge what an objective observer might think. He reached his conclusion in a time so short that he understood he had already known it. The context of political action and social change that the old men had struggled to outline had disappeared, and with it the story about the courage and perseverance of his father's generation, which he had hoped to tell. Instead, he had produced a gallery of entertaining characters, their features drawn as clearly as if he had asked them to act out the parts. There was a funny man, a romantic, a rogue, and someone else whose ludicrous argumentativeness had become a running theme. His father, too, had become a character in the show, aloof and a little enigmatic. Mr Mensah was right, Joseph thought bitterly, the whites would love it. There was nothing here to disturb the sleep of the great British public, no reflection of the anger and grief he had experienced while listening to the old men, and remembering Mr Mensah's smile he guessed they believed he had made a deliberate choice to misrepresent and trivialise them.

In that mood, he telephoned Kofi.

'I understand what Mr Mensah was trying to say.'

'Don't let it worry you.'

Joseph couldn't read his father's tone, but he knew that, somehow, he needed to explain. Without giving Kofi a chance to interrupt he began quickly to describe the long process of editing, and the way that the company exerted its control over the product.

'I would have done it differently if I could,' he ended.

'I know that,' Kofi said. 'We all knew that. The man who pays the piper gets to call the tune. That's what they say, and why would she want our version of a story she thinks she owns?' Joseph heard him chuckling down the line. 'None of us would have done any better. History is written by the winners. They will never allow you to say what they don't want to hear.'

Joseph guessed that these words were meant to be reassuring, but their cynicism didn't make him feel any better, partly because his unease was compounded by the sense that if he had fought harder he might have been able to preserve some of his original vision. To make matters worse, during some of his arguments with Hattie he had experienced the same feeling of powerlessness he used to feel in his quarrels with his mother. Some of it was due to the way she had always forced him to question himself and his own motives. Coming home with some story of a fight in the playground, or an insult in the classroom, she would look at him sternly – 'Are you sure you did nothing to provoke them?'

As he grew older he stopped talking to her about the anger and outrage he felt at these times. If his father had been there, he thought, he would have understood. As it was his mother's questions made him feel isolated and alone. Years later, as a resentful fifteen-year-old, he accused her of undermining his confidence and filling his mind with self-doubt. She'd heard him out with a puzzled frown. 'I didn't want you to be full of hate,' she said. 'Like your father.'

It was only after she died that, free of guilt, he allowed himself to know his father better. At that point he realised, with an odd pang of sorrow, how little she had understood about either of them. On the surface there was practically no resemblance between Hattie and his mum, but there had been times, while they wrangled about the editing, that he had seen the same look crossing her face. It was a look he had frequently seen on the faces of white people he knew well, an expression which hinted that whatever the problem was, he was somehow denying the fact that it was his own fault.

Joseph would have been too embarrassed to tell Kofi about any of this, so he accepted his father's implied rebuke in silence. Luckily, he had a couple of months' grace before the series was broadcast to reassemble his confidence, but apart from a couple of short newspaper features he hadn't been required to talk in any great detail until the World Service interview. By the time he was invited to the festival in Prague, he had almost forgotten the misery and embarrassment he had felt on the afternoon of the first preview.

Oddly enough, sitting in his hotel room in Holesovice he had been thinking about Mr Mensah. If what George said was all true, did his father's friends know? Why had Kofi never told him?

He leant over to pick up the telephone, but as he did so the volume of music outside increased another notch. He got up and pushed the window shut, then, glancing at the clock, realised that he had been sitting on the bed for more than half an hour. He moved quickly to the door, then slowed down, thinking about how to deal with George. He dialled London again. Still no answer. Perhaps, he thought, putting the phone down at last, the man might have got fed up waiting and left.

As he got out of the lift he was still torn between curiosity and a kind of reluctance to encounter George again. Instinctively he looked at the armchair, but now it had been turned round to face the room, and it was occupied by a bulky old man with a bald head and a bushy beard. Joseph felt a surge of relief, then a movement caught his eye and he saw George sitting at the bar waving at him, his hand raised above his head.

'I'm sorry,' Joseph said. 'I had some things to do.'

George shrugged.

'I understand.'

He rapped lightly on the bar.

'*Prosim. Slivovice.*'

'You're a Czech?' Joseph asked him.

George frowned, his mouth twisting a little, as if it was an unpleasant notion.

'Me? No.' He lowered his voice. 'I am German.'

'I thought your mother was Russian.'

'She is. But I was born in Berlin. East Berlin.'

'How come?'

The barmaid, a wispy blonde with a pale translucent skin, put two glasses in front of them, and he put a note on the counter. George slid off the stool and stood up, put some money on the counter and grunted something.

'What?'

'I say thank you to her. *Dekuju.*'

To Joseph it sounded like *dekweege*, and he repeated it to himself, testing the sound. George grinned at him and picked up his glass.

'Drink,' he announced. 'We go.'

'Wait a minute,' Joseph said. 'Go where? What are you talking about?'

'Home.' George's voice had lost all traces of uncertainty as if everything had been discussed and arranged. 'My wife Radka, and my son Serge. They are in Prague. Yes. You eat with us.'

'I don't think so,' Joseph told him.

He was confused again, because, in the last few minutes George had, somehow, subtly begun to take charge, in much the way he imagined an older brother would, as if Joseph had accepted the truth of his story, and as if, all of a sudden, they had an established and long-standing relationship.

'There is no problem,' George said. 'You come. You are my brother. My son you are his uncle. Yes? There is no problem.'

'I don't know that,' Joseph declared firmly. 'Even if what you say is true this is still weird. I phoned my father in London, but he wasn't in, and until I speak with him all bets are off. So cut the brotherhood shit till I know what's going on here.'

George frowned, listening intently, his lips moving fractionally, as if mouthing some of the words.

'I understand,' he said slowly. 'This is not easy for you. No one has told you. But for me, too. Because you are English you think this is some mad man from the East.'

'That's not it,' Joseph cut in quickly. 'That's not how I feel. Not the way you think.'

He was about to say that he was troubled and disturbed, that he couldn't begin to describe how he felt, but it struck him at the same time that to do so would be to enter George's story, to tell him that it was real. He stopped, uncertain how to proceed. George's eyes, he noted, a tremor starting somewhere inside his guts, were the same colour as his own. A few seconds passed while they stood staring at each other.

'So,' George said slowly. 'You come?'

THREE

George's car was a shiny dark-red Jaguar. It looked brand
new. The interior was lined with soft cream-coloured
leather into which Joseph sank, his muscles relaxing and
coming to rest by an instant reflex. Through the darkened
windows a premature twilight softened the harsh geometry
of the city's suburban fringe. Suddenly Joseph felt like a
part of the surroundings, gliding imperceptibly through
its streets, floating on a carpet whose discreet vibrations
filled him with a sense of power and command. As soon
as they'd got into the car the stereo had started up, playing
a Stevie Wonder album that Joseph remembered buying as
a teenager. George tapped his fingers on the wheel in time
to the music, looking round and smiling at Joseph, but for
a couple of minutes he said nothing.

In spite of his determination to maintain his distance,
Joseph found himself studying George's profile, searching
it for signs of a resemblance to himself or his father. He
was conscious of waiting for George to speak, to explain
more about who he was, how he had arrived at this time
and place, but in a few minutes he was also overwhelmed
by the ridiculousness of the situation. He looked round the
interior of the car again. There was no way, he thought,
that George could be a common or garden confidence
trickster. To drive a car like this he'd need to be making
some serious money.

'What do you do for a living?' Joseph asked, pitching his
voice above the music.

George grinned, as if the question amused him.

'Business. I'm a businessman.'

'All right,' Joseph said. 'What kind of business?'

'Business, you know. I buy. I sell. Only business.'

There was something final about the tone in which he said this, as if he had no intention of volunteering anything further, and Joseph tried another tack.

'How old are you?'

'I was born in 1958. In Berlin.'

That would make him four years older than Joseph.

'Is that where you live?'

George glanced sideways at Joseph, smiling reflectively, as if he understood the point of all these questions, and had no intention of giving too much away.

'Sometimes.'

His enigmatic manner had begun to drive Joseph to a high point of exasperation. He peered out of the window, trying to control his irritation. On their right was some sort of wood.

'Letinsky Sady,' George said when he saw Joseph looking.

'What?'

'Letna Park.'

It didn't look much like a park, Joseph told him. In England parks were man-made, manicured pieces of turf and garden reclaimed from the sprawling of cities. Even the royal parks, which had been there for a very long time, were designed and designated as places of leisure. In comparison Letinsky looked like a tract of forest which had somehow survived from prehistory, its tall dark trees climbing up a steep slope which was crowned by a rectangular block of rusting concrete. Even though they were close to the middle of the city the scene had a gloomy deserted air which made Joseph think of running wolves and bodies abandoned among the fallen leaves.

'When Michael Jackson came to Prague,' George said, 'he placed a big statue of himself here in the park.' Joseph peered out trying, without success, to imagine it. George nodded his head as if to emphasise a point. 'I was here. There were kids fucking everywhere under the trees. It was great. Before that they say there was a big statue of Stalin, the biggest in the world.' He looked round at Joseph, grinning. 'In those days nobody fucked without permission.'

It was easier to imagine Stalin's frown brooding over the dark wood.

'So what happened to it?'

'Oh, they exploded it many years ago.'

They had crossed a bridge, but they seemed to be climbing, going away from the centre of the city. Ahead of them reared a tower, three pillars of shiny metal like the needle noses of rockets thrusting upwards into the supine grey sky. Streaks of water, fine and delicate lines of wet beads, began tracing decorations along the outside of the glass.

'All year it rains in Prague,' George said.

'My father never lived in Berlin,' Joseph told him. 'In 1958 he was in London.'

'Yes,' George said. 'When I was born he was not there.'

He pulled over to the kerb and stopped. Peering out, Joseph saw that they were parked in a street where a gaggle of shopfronts alternated with offices and apartments, most of which seemed to be lined with scaffolding. Everywhere he went in the city it occurred to him, there was scaffolding. The façades of the building were usually long ruled blocks of plaster, like the grand streets of an English seaside town, but there was nothing elegant about them. Instead the surfaces were peeling and spotted, some of them with a bulging rotten look, as if only the grey piping of the scaffolding was holding the plaster in place.

Next to the car was a massive doorway faced with rusty metal. It was painted black, but the gloss was crumbling and peeling, the grey patches giving it a scaly, diseased air.

'We are here,' George announced. 'Come.'

Joseph got out of the car and looked over at George on the other side.

'I've gone far enough,' he said firmly. 'I'm going to take